A Visit to the Kingdom of Camelot

A Visit to the Kingdom of Camelot

R. L. Greenwood

iUniverse

A Visit to the Kingdom of Camelot

iUniverse books may be ordered through booksellers or by contacting:

iUniverse
1663 Liberty Drive
Bloomington, IN 47403
www.iuniverse.com
1-800-Authors (1-800-288-4677)

Because of the dynamic nature of the Internet, any Web addresses or
links contained in this book may have changed since publication and
may no longer be valid. The views expressed in this work are solely those
of the author and do not necessarily reflect the views of the publisher,
and the publisher hereby disclaims any responsibility for them.

Any people depicted in stock imagery provided by Thinkstock are models,
and such images are being used for illustrative purposes only.

Certain stock imagery © Thinkstock.

ISBN: 978-1-4759-8097-4 (sc)
ISBN: 978-1-4759-8098-1 (e)

Print information available on the last page.

iUniverse rev. date: 09/29/2015

It was my late sister-in-law, J. Sharron Clark, who first talked me into writing this story for her grandchildren. As such, this book is dedicated to her memory.

Camelot Gets a New King

In the kingdom of Camelot, there was a very old king. He was a good king, but he was a very old king, and one day he died. He had no son who could take his place. The knights, especially Sir Lancelot and Sir Gerwain, all wanted to become king, but they couldn't decide who it should be. Then Sir Lancelot had a good idea. They would ask the magician Merlin to decide for them. The knights put on their best armor and set off for Merlin's cabin in the woods.

Merlin was a wise old man who lived in the woods with his owl named Growl, who helped him. Growl the Owl also guarded Merlin from people who came to his cabin, because Merlin liked to be left alone. Whenever anyone came to see Merlin, Growl would bird bomb them. (This means that Growl pooped on their heads so they would go away.)

But the knights were not afraid of Growl because they were wearing their armor. They just covered their faces as they rode up to the cabin. Merlin heard all the noise that the owl was making and opened the door. When he saw the knights, he told Growl to stop. Growl flew up to the roof and just hooted at the knights.

Sir Lancelot was the first to speak. "Merlin, sir," he said, "we have a bad problem. The king is dead, and we can't decide who should be the next king."

Merlin pulled on his long white beard as he thought about the knights' problem. He called Growl down from the roof and told him all about it too. Growl hooted and hooted. Then Merlin said, "I have discussed this great problem with my friend here, and we have decided that we know the answer. Down by the lake, there is a big rock. Sticking out of the rock is the world's greatest magical sword. It is called Excalibur. Whoever holds this sword is a king. All you have to do is go down to the lake, and whoever pulls the sword from the stone will be king of Camelot."

The knights thought this was a good idea. They also needed to wash the owl poop off their armor. So they jumped on their horses and rushed down to the lake. They found the big rock, and, sure enough, there was Excalibur sticking out of it, just as Merlin had said. Sir Lancelot climbed on the rock and tugged and tugged on the handle of Excalibur. It would not come out of the rock. Sir Galahad tried to pull it out, but he couldn't move it even a little. Sir Gerwain, Sir Ivan, Sir Tyler, and all the other knights took a try, but they couldn't pull it out of the rock.

A young boy had been fishing in the lake. His name was Arthur, but everyone called him Artie. He watched what the knights were doing. At last he said to them, "Can I try to pull the sword out of the stone? I am pretty strong."

The knights all laughed and laughed at Artie. "How can a little squirt like you be stronger than all these great knights?" Sir Galahad told him to go away.

Artie pulls the sword from stone
and becomes King Arthur.

But Sir Lancelot said, "No! Artie may not be very big, but he is a good boy and should be given a chance."

Sir Lancelot knew Artie and thought he would make a great knight when he got a little bigger. "You can try to pull out the sword, Artie, but try not to fall off the rock and hurt yourself."

So Artie climbed on the rock and grabbed the handle of Excalibur. Then a miracle happened! Artie seemed to grow taller, and Excalibur started to glow. Artie pulled Excalibur out of the rock and held it above his head.

The knights were amazed; Arthur was the new king of Camelot. Each dropped down on one knee, because that was the way you greeted a king in those days.

Arthur was a good king. He made sure that all the knights helped him when he had a meeting at his famous Round Table. King Arthur decided that all of his knights would be equal to him, so he had them sit around a round table, so that no one would be the head. They would all have an equal voice in their decisions. His favorite and most loyal knight was Sir Lancelot, who was a great knight. He had long blond hair that came right down to his shoulders. He rode his big white horse all over Camelot, doing work for King Arthur.

But what no one knows is that Sir Lancelot had a little brother. When Sir Lancelot's brother was born, he was named Ellsworth. When Ellsworth was a baby, his mother fed him one day and put him on her shoulder to burp him. He **BURPED!** His **BURP** was so big and strong it blew a window out of the castle. King Arthur was angry. Windows were hard to get, since they had to be brought to Camelot on horseback from far away and cost a lot of money. So King Arthur made a law that any time Ellsworth had to be burped, he had to be pointed away from any window.

One day after Ellsworth gave a big **BURP,** his nurse said, "His brother is Lancelot. We should call him 'Burpsalot,' because that is what he does all the time." Everyone in the castle agreed. From that day on, no one called him Ellsworth; he became just plain Burpsalot.

As time went on, Burpsalot grew up and one day he was called into the castle to see King

Burpsalot burps and blows the
window out of the castle.

Arthur. King Arthur said to him, "You have grown up, and it is time you became a knight like your big brother, Sir Lancelot. So today I am making you a knight. You will now be known as Sir Burpsalot, because that is what you do."

One day King Arthur got a visit from one of his subjects. The man was a farmer who raised sheep on his farm. But the farmer was having trouble. There was a dragon near his farm that was eating his sheep. The farmer asked King Arthur to get rid of the dragon.

King Arthur knew this was really bad. He sent a messenger to find his greatest knight, who was his best dragon fighter: Sir Lancelot. Sir Lancelot came rushing in to see the king. King Arthur said, "All of this poor man's sheep are being eaten by a nasty, fire-breathing dragon. Can you get rid of this awful dragon?"

Sir Lancelot stood up very straight and said, "I am the best dragon killer in the world. I will get rid of him."

So Sir Lancelot set off on his beautiful white horse to do battle with the nasty dragon. He looked very handsome, with his straight back and his beautiful long blond hair that hung right down past his shoulders.

The next day Sir Lancelot came back to see King Arthur. He looked terrible. His beautiful blond hair was all burned off. He had no eyebrows. And he was very sad. The dragon had even burned the tail and mane straight off his horse. Sir Lancelot said to King Arthur, "I am sorry, Your Majesty, but I could not defeat this dragon. He breathes fire, and I could not get close enough to slay him."

King Arthur was very disappointed because he had promised the farmer that he would get rid of the nasty dragon. So King Arthur sent out a message to all his subjects to see if anyone could help him get rid of the dragon.

No one came to King Arthur with any ideas for quite a while. But finally Sir Burpsalot went to King Arthur and said, "I would like to get rid of this bad dragon for you. I have a good idea and will leave tomorrow to take care of this bad, sheep-eating dragon." So King Arthur told him he should go ahead.

Sir Burpsalot left the king and went to his room. He did not BURP, and when he went downstairs for his supper, he did not BURP. Sir Burpsalot did not BURP after supper like he usually did. He just quit BURPING. All the people in the castle realized that since Sir Burpsalot was no longer BURPING, there was no danger of the windows being blown out, and people no longer had to worry about having their hair blown off when Sir Burpsalot was around. But they also noticed that Sir Burpsalot was getting bigger. He got fatter and fatter all the time, and when he went to bed, he was blown up like a balloon.

The next morning when Sir Burpsalot woke up, he needed help to get out of bed. He did not BURP when he went downstairs for breakfast. He ate a big breakfast, but he still did not BURP. Then he went out into the castle yard and told the stable boy to bring the biggest horse in the stable. Sir Burpsalot had grown so big that he was four times his normal size. He could not get on his horse by himself. All the stable boys had to help him onto the big horse.

Sir Burpsalot rode out to meet the nasty, fire-breathing dragon. He had to have a stable boy on each side of him to make sure he stayed on the big horse, because he was still getting fatter all the time. But Sir Burpsalot did not BURP.

When Sir Burpsalot, with the stable boys, came up to the cave where the nasty, fire-breathing dragon lived, he fell off his horse and bounced on the ground like a rubber ball. The stable boys helped him stand up, and Sir Burpsalot walked up to the cave. The nasty dragon saw him coming and thought, *Here comes another stupid knight who thinks that he will slay me. I won't just burn off his hair and eyebrows; I will make toast out of him and have him for breakfast.*

The nasty dragon then threw back his head to send a great ball of fire at poor big fat Sir Burpsalot. But Sir Burpsalot was ready for him, and just when the dragon's head was reared back, Sir Burpsalot let go. It was the biggest B-U-R-R-R-R-P the world had ever heard before or ever has since. The BURP hit that nasty dragon right in the mouth and sent him back into the cave on his tail. The nasty dragon got up and looked at Sir Burpsalot, who was now back to his normal size. The dragon was no longer breathing fire. His fire was out. The dragon smiled at Sir Burpsalot and said, "Thank you,

Sir Burpsalot hits the dragon with a Burp
and sends him back into the cave.

Sir Knight. You have put out that fire that has been burning in my belly ever since I came to Camelot. It was making me very nasty because my belly always hurt. That is why I treated everyone so badly and tried to hurt them."

Sir Burpsalot looked at what had been a nasty, fire-breathing dragon and was very happy. The dragon was now smiling at him. Sir Burpsalot said, "It is no wonder you had a fire in your belly. You have been eating sheep and swallowed them with their wool on. The wool caught fire in your belly and made you nasty and mean. You will have to quit eating sheep."

So Sir Burpsalot gathered the farmers around the dragon's cave to bring him fruits and vegetables, so he would have lots to eat and would not eat their sheep. The dragon, whose name was George, became a great friend of Sir Burpsalot. He would carry Sir Burpsalot on his back as he flew all over Camelot. George liked having Sir Burpsalot with him when he went flying, because when the crows and eagles would attack poor George, Sir Burpsalot would let out one of his BURPS and blow them out of the sky. George the Dragon and Sir Burpsalot became King Arthur's greatest friend and knight.

Sir Lancelot's Sister Becomes an Expert Archer

O nce upon a time, long, long ago in the kingdom of Camelot ruled by the great King Arthur, the people were very happy.

The dragon that had been eating farmers' sheep was made tame by Sir Burpsalot, and they were good friends. Sir Burpsalot used to ride George the Dragon all over Camelot, and sometimes over other kingdoms around Camelot. Sir Burpsalot became a great knight, along with his brother, Sir Lancelot. King Arthur depended on them to solve any problems that sometimes bothered people.

The two knights had a younger sister named Wendy. Wendy watched her brothers practicing with their swords, bows, and arrows. She wanted to shoot arrows just like her brothers.

She was told, "Girls don't shoot arrows. Only boys and men are allowed to be knights, and only knights can shoot arrows. So you can't do it. You are just a girl."

"But that is not fair," Wendy said. "Girls should be able to shoot arrows, too."

She was told that it was just the way things were. Girls were supposed to stay in the castle and mend socks and learn to cook and do girl things.

Wendy was not happy. One day she watched her brothers shooting arrows. A page brought Sir Burpsalot a new bow made especially for him by King Arthur's best bow maker. Sir Burpsalot liked his new bow and threw his old bow in the trash can.

When Sir Burpsalot and Sir Lancelot left to go for a horseback ride, Wendy picked the bow out of the garbage and took it with her to her room. She looked at it every day and dreamed about shooting some arrows. One day she found some arrows that had been left behind after her brothers had finished their shooting practice. She went to her room and got the bow.

Wendy knew that she could not practice shooting her bow and arrows with her brothers, so she went out into the forest where no one could watch her. She set up a target and started shooting. At first, she couldn't even hit the target, but she kept trying and finally shot an arrow right into the center. Wendy got a bull's-eye!

From that day on, Wendy went into the forest every day and practiced shooting at her target. She got so she could hit a bull's-eye every time. She became an expert archer.

But Wendy was not happy. She could not shoot arrows with her brothers. Wendy went to talk to her mother, Lady Tanya, to ask her what she should do. Lady Tanya thought for a while and said, "I do not know what to tell you. I do not have an answer to such a hard question. Why don't you go and ask Merlin the Magician for his advice? He knows everything."

So Wendy set off to see Merlin the Magician, who lived in a cabin in the woods with his wise old owl, Growl. Growl's job was to keep people away so they wouldn't disturb him while he studied things. If they did, Growl would bird bomb them.

When Wendy walked toward the cabin, Growl saw her and flew over her head. Now, Growl's job was to guard Merlin's home and keep people away. But poor Growl did not know what to do this time. He had never seen a girl before, and this person was not wearing armor like the knights did. Instead, she wore a bright red dress and did not even have a hat, so Growl did not bird bomb her. He just hooted at her. He hooted and hooted.

Merlin came to the door to see what all the fuss was about and saw Wendy. "What can I do for you, little lady?" he asked.

"Oh, Mr. Merlin, sir, my name is Wendy, and I have a big problem. I am a great archer, but I can't let anyone see me shoot any arrows because I am a girl."

Merlin thought about Wendy's problem for a long time. He called Growl to discuss it with him. Growl hooted and hooted, and finally Merlin said, "Miss Wendy, I think you should go back into the woods behind the cabin. Growl will show you the way. He will take you to see Lucy. She is a unicorn. You will recognize her when you see her because she looks like a horse but has a horn sticking out right in the middle of her forehead. She also has wings and she can fly. Lucy will be able to help you."

"But horses can't talk," Wendy said.

"Unicorns are not horses," said Merlin. "They are magical animals who talk just like you and me."

So Wendy followed Growl deep into the forest, and they soon found Lucy.

"What do you want?" asked Lucy, not very nicely.

"Good unicorn, my name is Wendy, and I have a big problem."

Wendy told Lucy her problem, and Lucy listened to every word before she spoke.

Wendy meets Lucy the unicorn who
shows her how she can fly.

"I know that some people cannot accept that some girls are different and want to do things that other people are not used to. I can fly and talk like everyone else, but people do not like that, so I just stay away from them. I think I can help you. Get on my back and hold on to my mane. I will take you to someone who makes screaming arrows that will make people pay attention to you. Screaming arrows make so much noise that they hurt people's ears and make them want to hide."

So Wendy got on Lucy's back, and they flew up over a mountain. They landed in another forest, near a tiny cabin.

"This is the home of Twerp," said Lucy. "He makes the screaming arrows."

Lucy thumped on the door with her hoof, and Twerp answered it. Lucy told Twerp about Wendy and how she needed some screaming arrows.

Twerp said, "I don't let just anyone have my screaming arrows unless they promise not to shoot anyone with them. They are a secret weapon that only certain people are allowed to have. You look like a nice young lady who would not hurt anyone, so I will give you some."

Wendy took a whole bundle of screaming arrows and got back on the unicorn's back. They flew back over the trees and the mountain, back to the castle in Camelot, where they saw Wendy's brothers practicing their archery. She put a screaming arrow in her bow and shot it at their target. She made a bull's-eye. The arrow scared both Sir Lancelot and Sir Burpsalot and really hurt their ears. When they looked up into the sky, they saw Wendy on the back of a beautiful white unicorn. They did not know what to say. Wendy just flew off laughing on Lucy's back.

From that day on, Wendy was allowed to shoot arrows with her brothers because they were afraid that she might shoot another screaming arrow near them.

Wendy was happy now. Her new friend, Lucy, would come to see her often, and they would go flying together. Sometimes Sir Burpsalot would get on the back of his friend George, the friendly dragon, and they would fly all over the countryside together.

Wendy gets her brother's attention
with a screaming arrow.

Wendy and Sir Burpsalot Meet the Stinkers

One really hot day Wendy went to see Sir Burpsalot, who was busy practicing his swordsmanship.

"Sir Burpsalot, it is so hot, why don't we get George the Dragon and my unicorn Lucy and fly up into the clouds, where it will be cooler?"

Sir Burpsalot thought this was a good idea, so he set off on his horse to George's den. George was also very hot and thought it was a good idea. So Sir Burpsalot got on the dragon's back and flew back to the castle, where Wendy was waiting with Lucy.

"Where should we go?" asked Sir Burpsalot.

"I would like to fly over those mountains," said Wendy. "They are so high that it is sure to be cool up there, and we have never seen what is on the other side."

Sir Burpsalot agreed and off they went. They flew higher and higher, and it got cooler and cooler. Soon they were over the tops of the mountains and saw a beautiful valley. They decided they would land and talk to the people who lived in this new kingdom. When they came down to the ground, there was a terrible smell.

"What is that awful stink?" asked Wendy.

"I don't know," said Sir Burpsalot, "but I will ask about it from the first person we see."

They flew along over the ground and finally saw a little lady. She was half the size of Wendy, but she had gray hair like a grandmother should. She was not a little kid.

"Excuse me, madam. What kingdom are we in, and what is that terrible smell you have here?" asked Burpsalot.

The lady introduced herself. "My name is Frizzytop," she said. "I do not like that name, so I always put a lot of fat from my pigs on my head to make my hair lay down. But they still call me Frizzytop. You are in the Kingdom of Tooters, and that terrible smell is coming from those terrible Stinkers," she said. "Stinkers look like little balls of pink hair with long noses that they can turn inside out so they don't smell anything bad. They live just over those hills, and they keep stealing our stuff."

"What do you mean, they keep stealing your stuff?" asked Wendy.

"Well, they come over those hills and throw stink bombs at us. The smell is so bad that it makes us sick, so we run away and hide in the hills until they leave. While we are gone, they come and steal everything they find. Can you help us get rid of these pests?"

"What do you think, Sir Burpsalot?" asked Wendy.

"I think this calls for us to teach these stinking people a lesson so they will not come back," said Sir Burpsalot. "Jump on Lucy and I will get on

George, and we will chase them back to their own stinking place, where they belong."

So they asked their new friend when the Stinkers might attack them next with their stink bombs.

"We will know when they are getting close," said Frizzytop. "We will be able to hear the Poodletooters."

"What are the Poodletooters?" asked Wendy.

"They are our pets. A Poodletooter looks like a poodle but has a long nose that acts like a horn. When the Poodletooters are not watching the border for us, they play music with their noses for us. They are at the border now, and we will hear them tooting when the Stinkers invade," said Frizzytop.

Just then they heard a lot of tooting. It was very loud and it sounded like a thousand trumpets.

"The Stinkers are coming. Run away or you will be very sick," said Frizzytop.

"I am not letting those Stinkers chase me away," said Sir Burpsalot. "Let's get them and chase them back home where they belong."

So Wendy and Sir Burpsalot got on the unicorn and the dragon and flew over the area where the greatest stink was coming from. There they saw a bunch of little, round, roly-poly people marching toward the border of this beautiful country. They were carrying things that looked like a lot of stink bombs.

"Let's stop them in their tracks," said Sir Burpsalot. "Send them a screaming arrow right in the middle of their army."

So Wendy put a screaming arrow in her bow. It landed right in the middle of the Stinker army. It was so noisy that the Stinkers covered their ears and fell to the ground; it hurt that bad.

"Send them back home," said Wendy. "Hit them with a BIG BURP, and make them roll."

So Sir Burpsalot let go with a BIG BURP he had been holding all day for just this moment. He burped so hard that it hit the Stinkers right in the middle of their army, and they all rolled back

Wendy and Sir Burpsalot chase the
Stinkers back home to their Kingdom.

home. Wendy and Sir Burpsalot followed them back over the border and then flew down over them to let them know they were not welcome back again.

"Stay in your own kingdom!" shouted Wendy. "If we see you near the border again, we will come back and hurt your ears even worse."

Wendy and Burpsalot then flew back to see Frizzytop, who thanked them for saving them from the Stinkers. She promised to send them a message if the Stinkers came back again.

Wendy and Burpsalot then flew home and were very happy with their trip.

Back to the Land of the Stinkers

One day Wendy was in the castle helping her mother, Lady Tanya, mend the holes in the knights' socks. She was bored.

"I do not like this job," she said.

Her mother agreed that it was a boring job but said it had to be done. She also said that Wendy should go outside and get some fresh air and exercise. So Wendy went outside, where she met her brother, Sir Burpsalot.

"Why don't we fly over to the Kingdom of Tooters to see if the Stinkers are behaving themselves?" she said.

"Good idea," said Sir Burpsalot. "I will go and get George the Dragon, and you get Lucy the Unicorn."

So the brother and sister set off and were soon flying over the mountains and forests to the Kingdom of Tooters. They flew down to their friend Frizzytop's house. She saw them coming and rushed out to greet them when they landed. She knew she did not need to be afraid of the dragon or the unicorn, for she had learned that they were friends, too.

"Are the Stinkers behaving themselves?" asked Wendy.

"Yes and no," said Frizzytop. "They no longer bring stink bombs into our kingdom to make us sick. They decided after you chased them all home that they had to change their ways. So instead of making stink bombs in their factories, they are now making perfume."

"That sounds like a much better idea," said Wendy.

"Well, yes, they are no longer invading us, but they come over the border to sell us their perfumes. Now they stink of perfume. They put so much on all over themselves that we have to hold our noses when we go to buy it from them. They are still Stinkers. At least they no longer make us sick. They are also selling their perfumes to other kingdoms, and they make enough money that they don't have to steal from us," said Frizzytop.

"Let's go to see the Stinkers and see what they are doing," said Sir Burpsalot. "Let's see if we can find someone to talk to."

So Sir Burpsalot and Wendy flew over to the Kingdom of Stinkers. They landed in a beautiful field of flowers.

"This is what the Stinkers are using to make their perfume. We must be very careful not to do damage any of these beautiful, fragrant flowers," said Wendy.

No one came to greet them, but they saw the little pink Stinkers peeking at them from everywhere. "Why don't they come out to greet us?" asked Sir Burpsalot.

"They are afraid of George the Dragon and Lucy the Unicorn," Wendy said. "I will get someone to come to talk to us." Wendy made a big sign that read: "WE WANT TO BUY SOME PERFUME."

Finally a little, pink, roly-poly, fuzzy Stinker came out from behind her house and waddled up to them. "My name is Sharoom. I will sell you some perfume."

So Wendy and Sir Burpsalot each bought a big bottle of perfume to take home to Camelot.

On the way home Wendy said, "We have to make sure when we give this to the people of Camelot, they use it properly. We don't want them smelling like Stinkers."

Sir Burpsalot agreed, and said, "I will not pass it out to the knights, even if they always smell of horses. Knights smelling like horses is better than them smelling of stinky perfume. I think that this perfume stuff stinks, and it always makes me sneeze. My sneezes are almost as dangerous as my burps. The last time I sneezed, I blew a hole in the castle wall."

Wendy buys some purfume from the Stinkers.

So Wendy and Sir Burpsalot flew back home to Camelot with perfume for everyone. The people of Camelot used it right and did not become Stinkers.

Wendy and Sir Burpsalot Go to Beanland

One day much later, Wendy went out into the castle courtyard to go for a walk. She ran into her brother Sir Burpsalot.

"What are you doing today?" she asked.

"Nothing much. Sir Lancelot is away doing some business for King Arthur, and so I am not doing any knight training today," answered Sir Burpsalot.

"Why don't we go and see how the Stinkers are doing?" asked Wendy.

"Good idea," said Sir Burpsalot. "I will go and get George, and you get Lucy, and we will take off."

Soon they were riding the bright, fresh air over the now-familiar mountains and across fields and fields of flowers. They landed in the Kingdom of Stinkers and soon saw Sharoom, the roly-poly Stinker they had met earlier.

Sharoom rushed to meet them. "Do you want to buy some perfume?" she asked.

"Not today," said Wendy. "We still have lots left in the bottles we bought the last time we were here. How is the perfume selling now?"

"We are selling a lot of it now, especially in the Kingdom of Beanland," said Sharoom. "You should go and see this beautiful kingdom."

So Wendy and Sir Burpsalot got back on their animal friends' backs and flew over the hills to the Kingdom of Beanland. They did not expect to see what they saw! Instead of fields of green and yellow beans, they saw what looked like rainbows everywhere. The beautiful fields were of all colors. Red, green, pink, yellow, purple, and orange pods adorned the plants. It was a field of jelly beans!

As Wendy and Sir Burpsalot looked around, they saw that the houses were all decorated with jelly beans and were also beautiful.

"This is strange," said Wendy, "but I sure like it. Let's find someone to talk to."

They walked down a road that was lined with posts made from jelly beans. They saw a lady coming down this road. Jelly bean necklaces circled her throat in red, yellow, pink, purple, and white, and jelly bean bracelets decorated both arms.

"Hello!" she said. "I am Rainbow. Who are you? And what are those animals you are riding? They are scary."

"We are Wendy and Sir Burpsalot. I ride a unicorn and Sir Burpsalot rides a dragon. They are our best friends, and you do not have to be afraid of them."

Just then Wendy noticed a beautiful big butterfly. "What a beautiful butterfly!" she said.

"That is not a butterfly," said Rainbow. "It is not made of butter, and it does not eat butter. What a silly name for it! That is a 'flutterby,' because that is what they do. They love our fields of jelly beans. We do not have bees in Beanland, so we need our flutterbys to pollinate our jelly bean crop," said Rainbow.

"You sure have a lot of jelly beans. Why do you grow so many?" asked Wendy.

"They are the only thing we eat. Our jelly beans have all the things we need to stay healthy and are not like the jelly beans most people in other countries have. They are found only here. We carry them around our necks and arms for lunch wherever we go," said Rainbow.

"But I don't see any black ones," said Wendy. "Why don't you grow them?"

"We do! But all our black jelly beans are stolen by the crows, who eat them to keep their feathers shiny and black. It is terrible because we need them too. They are part of our diet and help us to stay healthy," said Rainbow.

"Where do the crows come from?" asked Wendy.

"They live on that mountain with an old, nasty crone we call 'Beaky.' She sends them down to our fields. She has the best place to grow black jelly beans, but she no longer grows them, since she is too old to plant a garden," said Rainbow.

"Let's go up and talk to her," said Sir Burpsalot.

Wendy and Sir Burpsalot got on their friends' backs and flew up toward the mountaintop. A large flock of crows came out to meet them. They wanted to chase George the Dragon. Sir Burpsalot let go with a big **BURP** and blew them out of the air. Wendy and Sir Burpsalot landed in the old crone's yard, and the crows just sat in the trees and cawed at the visitors.

The old crone came to the door of her cabin to see what all the fuss was about. She saw the dragon and the unicorn and their two riders in her yard, and she was afraid.

"Don't be afraid," said Wendy. "These are our friends, and they will not hurt you. We have come to talk to you about growing some black jelly beans here. Should we call you Beaky?"

"Those flatlanders call me that, but my real name is Becky. I do not like being called Beaky, even though I have a big, long nose," said Becky.

Sir Burpsalot said, "Would you agree to let the people from the flatlands plant you a garden of black beans? You would also have to make sure the crows do not eat them all. You must leave lots of the black jelly beans for the people who plant them and really need them."

"Oh yes," said Becky. "I would like that."

So Sir Burpsalot and Wendy flew back down to talk to Rainbow. They told her about the arrangement they had made with Becky. Rainbow thought this was a good idea.

Wendy and Sir Burpsalot loaded the black jelly bean seed on the backs of George and Lucy and took the seeds to the top of the mountain, so they would be ready to plant. Rainbow gathered

Wendy and Sir Burpsalot make a deal with
Becky to grow black jelly beans on her place.

Wendy and Sir Burpsalot go to see
Becky and her jelly bean eating crows.

her friends and neighbors together and went up the mountain to plant the black jelly beans.

Everyone was happy, and soon there would be plenty of nutritious black jelly beans for everyone, including Becky's crows.

Sir Burpsalot
Becomes a King

The next year, King Arthur sent a messenger to Sir Burpsalot to come to the castle for a meeting.

Sir Burpsalot was excited to meet the king, thinking that he would get a new job. He rushed to the castle after he put on his best clothes and made sure his hair was brushed and combed. King Arthur appeared very pleased to see him and said that he indeed had an important proposal for Sir Burpsalot.

"I have had a visit from the king of Avalon. He told me his daughter, Princess Keara, needs a husband to help her rule the kingdom after he retires," said King Arthur. "He wants someone who has proven to be a good leader and can work with other people to solve their problems. You have shown me that you can do this by your work with the Poodletooters, the Stinkers, and the people of Beanland. Your great weapon, your big BURP, could also be useful. You are to go to the kingdom of Avalon and meet with the king and the princess. If you like the princess and agree to marry her, you could become king of Avalon."

Sir Burpsalot was very excited at this news. He left the castle and went directly to tell George, the friendly dragon, all about it.

"I think I will be moving to Avalon," said Sir Burpsalot. "Will you move with me?"

"I am glad you came to see me," said George. "I have had a visit from a dragonfly. He brought me a message from my family that they need me, so I will be going home to where all the dragons live and will have a long visit."

"I didn't know you talked to dragonflies," said Sir Burpsalot.

"Oh yes, they speak the dragon language, and we often use them as messengers," said George. "So I will be going home soon and will not be able to go with you to Avalon. I have enjoyed our friendship. If you ever need my help again, just tell a dragonfly, and he will bring me the message."

Sir Burpsalot was sad to say good-bye to his friend and to his sister, Wendy. He left immediately for the kingdom of Avalon to meet the princess. He hoped she would not be ugly and that she had a happy personality. He rode up to the castle of Avalon and asked a guard to see the princess.

The castle was expecting him, and he was taken to a big room where Princess Keara was waiting for him. She was very beautiful, and Sir Burpsalot immediately fell in love with her smile. He took her hand and said, "Let's go see your father."

Sir Burpsalot liked the king of Avalon as soon as he met him. "I would like to marry your daughter," he said.

"You are very highly regarded by King Arthur, and we welcome you to Avalon to come and live in our kingdom and marry the princess. Are you also prepared to become king and help her rule the kingdom when I retire?" asked the king.

Sir Burpsalot was indeed agreeable to the king's wish. So he and Keara became engaged and made plans for him to move to Avalon, where he eventually became king.

Sir Burpsalot meets and falls in
love with Princess Keara.

Wendy Gets a New Job

When King Arthur heard that Sir Burpsalot and Princess Keara were engaged, he was very happy. He called his knights together around the Round Table to help him make arrangements for a celebration. He sent a messenger to Avalon to ask the young couple to come and join them.

Everyone in Camelot gathered in the castle, wearing their best clothes, to greet Sir Burpsalot and Princess Keara. The special guests arrived. They were very handsome and looked wonderful.

As Sir Burpsalot walked around with Princess Keara to introduce her to his friends and family, King Arthur noticed that Wendy did not look happy. "What is wrong, young lady?" he asked. "You do not seem to be enjoying this party."

"I am sad because my brother, and best friend, is leaving to move to Avalon. Although I am happy for him and love Princess Keara, I am sorry to see him leave."

King Arthur said gently, "So you are." He paused a moment, took her hand, and then said, "I would like you to meet Queen Eugenia, who is a special guest at this party. She is a great leader in her kingdom of Exeter. Her kingdom is always being attacked by vicious raiders from afar. She leads an army that chases them away all the time. She needs you and your screaming arrows to help her make her kingdom peaceful."

King Arthur took Wendy's hand and led her over to meet Queen Eugenia. Wendy liked her immediately and was impressed by her. Wendy saw a big, strong lady who, she was sure, was a great warrior.

When Queen Eugenia met Wendy she said, "King Arthur has told me all about you and your screaming arrows. I am sure you can help us. I hope you will be able to teach my twin sons, Prince Kaelan and Prince Cale, to use them as well."

Wendy agreed to help Queen Eugenia, but before she left for the kingdom of Exeter, she went to tell Lucy the Unicorn. Lucy listened to what Wendy told her and said, "I am sorry, Wendy, but you will have to go without me. I want to go back to live among the unicorns and spend some time with my family. But if you ever need me, just send me a message through Merlin the Magician. He will know how to reach me."

Wendy said a sad good-bye to her dear friend and then hurried to the castle to get ready for her trip to the kingdom of Exeter. When she arrived there, she was made minister of defense and soon became very well thought of and respected.

And Wendy lived happily ever after in her new home.